A Christmas Wish for Trafalgar Bear

Jenny Stevens

Illustrations by Elly Eveleigh

Published by New Generation Publishing in 2019

Copyright © Jenny Stevens 2019
Illustrations by Elly Eveleigh

First Edition

ISBN:
Paperback 978-1-78955-709-1
Hardback 978-1-78955-710-7

www.newgeneration-publishing.com

New Generation Publishing

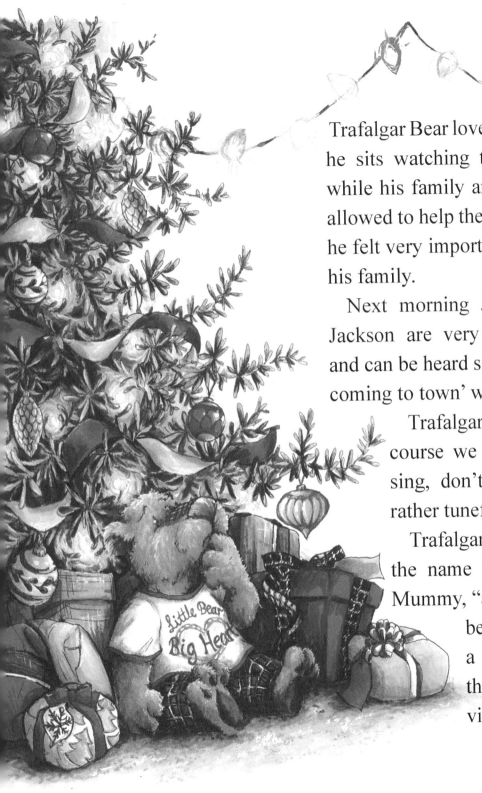

Trafalgar Bear loves the Christmas tree lights, he sits watching them twinkle in the dark while his family are asleep upstairs. He was allowed to help the boys decorate the tree and he felt very important and of course loved by his family.

Next morning Jonathan and his brother Jackson are very excited about Christmas and can be heard singing about 'Santa Clause coming to town' while they clean their teeth.

Trafalgar hums along with them, of course we all know that bears can't sing, don't we? But they can hum, rather tunefully too.

Trafalgar (now called 'T Bear' as the name Trafalgar is, according to Mummy, "a bit of a mouthful") has been told that he should make a Christmas wish tonight at the carol-singing around the village Christmas tree.

1

So today, while the boys are at school and Mummy and Nana Jenny are doing last-minute Christmas shopping, he will think carefully about his wish. He is full of ideas and spends the day sitting under the Christmas tree dreaming about his wish and what it should be.

While the family have tea later on Mummy explains about the family tradition. She often talks to T Bear, and she will explain this if asked – she says that Nana Jenny talks to her cats Ruby and Alfie all the time and no one raises an eyebrow, so talking to a furry, stuffed, toy bear is quite acceptable isn't it?

Every Christmas, a big Christmas tree is put up in the centre of the village and strung with hundreds of bright lights. All the villagers meet around the tree just before Christmas to sing carols and they write wishes on small red cardboard labels and tie them to the tree. Mummy says that on Christmas Eve the wishes are collected by the Christmas Wish Fairy who makes the wishes come true.

Nana Jenny arrives with an early Christmas gift for T Bear, a beautiful new blue coat to wear to the carol-singing. No one sees him smiling, although Nana Jenny does suspect that he is a 'special' bear and tickles him under his chin and gives him a kiss on his soft, furry head while she helps him into his new coat.

There is frost on the ground as the family make their way to the village square. People are already standing around the tree, they are all wrapped up warmly with brightly coloured hats, scarves and gloves. Everyone looks very splendid, thinks T Bear. There are lots of hugs and kisses and the new blue coat is much admired by everyone, T Bear blushes but is pleased that everyone thinks he looks so smart.

The village brass band play, their musical instruments shining in the light from the street lamps and the tree, and the people sing carols. It is all over far too quickly.

The Christmas wishes are written on red Christmassy labels and tied to the tree with string. They are secret of course, "otherwise they won't come true," explains Jonathan as he ties T Bear's wish to the tree.

Wanda the Christmas Wish Fairy, so named because of her sparkly wand and because she would wander here and there, sits on top of the village Christmas tree. She catches Trafalgar Bear's watchful eye and gives him a cheeky wink and one of her special Christmas Wish Fairy smiles.

Trafalgar's fur tingled, he had a good feeling about the wish labels that were hanging from the tree – would his wish be granted tonight on Christmas Eve?

After a mug of hot chocolate with marshmallows and a mince pie, everyone happily makes their way home, watched over by the Christmas Wish Fairy.

6

You might be wondering why Trafalgar Bear is so well known in the village?

A few weeks before Christmas Jonathan's teacher, Miss Sykes, had asked if anyone had a teddy bear that could take part in the school's nativity play. Of course Trafalgar Bear was volunteered and his whimsical smile and soft curly fur won the day – he was signed up.

Miss Sykes had decided to do a nativity with a difference this year, bringing it more up-to-date. She was slightly worried how it would be received by the parents – I wonder what you think about it?

She was replacing the gifts brought by the 3 wise men, no Gold, Frankincense or Myrrh but a teddy bear, a teething ring and some nursery rhyme books. Doubts pushed aside, the rehearsals went ahead and everyone was excited about the play, including

Trafalgar Bear whose ears twitched an awful lot.

On the night of the play, T Bear wore his best and favourite tee shirt – it was white with red writing saying 'Little bear with a big heart' on the front.

Jonathan who was Balthasar (one of the 3 wise men visiting the baby) was dressed in a purple and gold robe with a golden crown that wobbled about on his head. He looked very regal as he

proudly presented the baby Jesus with Trafalgar Bear and placed him in the crib. Trafalgar Bear thought the straw was a little itchy. Everyone clapped as the 3 unusual gifts were given and Miss Sykes breathed a sigh of relief.

A cow, a sheep and a donkey stood nearby, well actually Adam, Charlotte and Jackson wearing very life-like masks. Trafalgar Bear winked at them, but they did not wink back at him as they were taking their parts very seriously, or maybe a teddy bear winking at you was just not possible?

The play got a standing ovation and the little bear with the big heart felt very proud to have been a part of it, however small.

So this is why he is such a celebrity in the village.

"Tomorrow is Christmas day," Jonathan tells T Bear, "we can unwrap the presents," he says pointing at a brightly wrapped box with a red shiny bow on it. "That's your present, I hope you will like it?" Jonathan gives him a hug and goes to bed. T Bear doesn't think he can wait until tomorrow morning to unwrap his present, but he knows he must, "no sleep for me tonight he murmurs," a big bear-like smile on his face, his ears twitching with excitement.

I am guessing you would like to know what T Bear's Christmas wish was, and did it come true?

Even though he has a family who love him, T Bear still dreams about his London friends

– Pedro, Rebel, Dunbar, Sunny – and how he would love to meet them again. His adventures in London have never been forgotten, so his Christmas wish was to see his friends once again. I think we all knew that was his wish?

It is Christmas Eve.

Sitting on the window sill looking into the garden, a white winter frost covering the ground, T Bear is suddenly amazed to see footprints on the white, glistening grass. Then as if by magic he sees his London friends below the window, waving and jumping up and down with excitement.

Dunbar is wearing a bright red bandana adorned with silver Christmas trees, Sunny has a striped multi-coloured scarf around his neck with a sprig of mistletoe in it, Pedro and Rebel? Well they are as usual looking in fine fettle if not a little cold. They were stamping their feet because unlike the other two they do not have fur to keep them warm.

T Bear lets his friends into the kitchen, but just as he is going to close the door a small black bundle of wet fur streaks into the kitchen behind the four friends.

There are hugs all round and everyone is talking, asking questions and making T Bear chuckle. His friends all admire his PJs that are decorated with teddy bears.

"Very smart and cosy," declares Pedro,

who is secretly quite envious of the fashion-conscious bear's outfit.

Can you imagine it? I can.

T Bear suddenly notices the black, furry animal who is shivering in the corner of the kitchen. "Oh that is Boris," said Pedro. "He is a Rattus Rattus," explains Rebel. "He is a rat, plain and simple," said Dunbar. Boris pulled a face not happy being called a 'plain' rat, he thought himself rather regal because "I live in Buckingham Palace," he mutters as if to himself but making sure everyone hears him "How grand," says T Bear, who remembered visiting the Palace with Pedro. "Do you entertain the Queen?" he asked. Boris gave the question much thought, he was enjoying being the centre of attention and his

long, thick tail twitched as did his shiny whiskers.  "Oh no, I entertain the palace cats, I keep them busy playing hide and seek." Everyone laughed, picturing the fine specimen of Rattus Rattus being chased around the palace by the out-of-breath royal cats, the Queen quite unaware of the activity going on right underneath her nose. "They never catch me you know I am far too fast," he said as he puffed out his chest with self-importance and gave a rather ratty giggle.

They made an enchanting group of friends and T Bear felt very lucky that they have come all the way from London to visit him  on this cold Christmas Eve. He thought he could kiss the Christmas Wish Fairy for her kindness.

It was lovely and warm in the kitchen, the Christmas tree lights twinkled through the door from the lounge. "It's very festive," says Dunbar, "we have a Christmas tree in the pub and I sleep underneath it after I have been out hunting mice." Boris is not sure this is the true meaning of Christmas spirit, after all some of his best friends are mice, but he says nothing as it would be rude. He was after all a visitor and despite being a 'mere' rat he did have impeccable manners, which is only what is expected of a royal rat.

The friends exchange adventures.

Pedro has been back to Spain for a holiday to escape the cold and wet weather in London.

Sunny has been busy learning new tricks with his street entertainer friend. The tourists, in London to do their Christmas shopping, love him and he is quite famous in Covent Garden now.

And Rebel? Well he has been busy

guarding the Tower of London. "Just doing my job," he says but he did look proud and rightly so thought T Bear, it is a very important job.

Dunbar just muttered "same old, same old" and winked at T Bear, who wondered exactly what that meant but was sure it was properly exciting anyway.

The friends accepted the offer of mince pies, except Dunbar who had eaten far too many pies over the festive season and was all pied-out apparently. T Bear wondered how he would

explain the missing pies tomorrow and thought he might be in trouble, Christmas or no Christmas.

"My goodness," exclaimed Rebel, "how time flies," he laughed at his joke and ruffled his feathers, "we must be on our way," and they trudged out into the cold night air, waving as they walk across the frosty-white grass.

T Bear thinks it has been a truly magical visit. He wishes them all a Happy Christmas and waves back to them, sad to see his friends go but warm and happy inside and out.

Next morning when he woke up, T Bear remembered the night's adventures. He shook his head and wondered if it was all a dream? Had his Christmas wish come true?

He looked out of the window but there were no tiny footprints left on the lawn. 'Was it my imagination?' he wondered.

Dream or no dream, he felt very happy, "full of Christmas spirit" as Nana Jenny would have said.

He could hear Mummy grumbling in the kitchen, "where have all the mince pies gone? I am sure I had 2 tins full of them yesterday," she says. "Perhaps the Christmas Wish Fairy ate them," says daddy, laughing.

"Everyone downstairs, it's time to unwrap the presents," says Daddy. T Bear comes downstairs in Jonathan's arms, he was trying really hard to look innocent but if bears could blush he would have pink cheeks about now. He did a quick check to make sure there were no mince pie crumbs around his mouth or on his nose.

The boys were hopping up and down with excitement at the prospect of finding out what was in the beautifully wrapped presents that Father Christmas had delivered.

T Bear had help opening his present. Inside the box nestling in silver tissue paper is a soft, warm, multi-stripped scarf, "knitted by Nana Jenny, especially for you," says Jonathan, "and I chose the coloured wool." It was exactly the same as the one Sunny the street entertainer's dog was wearing last night.

So was it a dream or had the friends really come to visit him? We can only wonder.

"Happy Christmas," said Jonathan, hugging T Bear tight. Well it certainly is, thinks T Bear smiling from ear to ear, remembering the memories from the last few days – carols round the Christmas tree and a reunion with his London friends, a Christmas to remember.

But a question is still not answered – was it a dream or did his Christmas wish really come true?

Only the Christmas Wish Fairy knows the answer to that question.

"Happy Christmas to all my friends," says T Bear, snuggling into his Christmas scarf, smiling his happy bear smile.

Lightning Source UK Ltd.
Milton Keynes UK
UKHW050637231222
414294UK00003B/9